The Chicken Cat

BY STEPHANIE SIMPSON MCLELLAN

*May you find the
things in life that
you were born for!*

ILLUSTRATED BY SEAN CASSIDY

Fitzhenry & Whiteside

For Jeff, Sarah, Erin, Tristan and Merlin,
without whom this story wouldn't be.
Stephanie

To Sylvia and Maggie,
with whom all good things begin.
Sean

Text copyright © 2001 by Stephanie Simpson McLellan
Illustrations copyright © 2001 by Sean Cassidy

Published in Canada by Fitzhenry & Whiteside, 195 Allstate Parkway, Markham, Ontario L3R 4T8

Published in the United States by Fitzhenry & Whiteside, 311 Washington Street, Brighton, Massachusetts 02135

10 9 8 7 6 5 4 3 2

National Library of Canada Cataloguing in Publication Data

McLellan, Stephanie Simpson, 1959-
The chicken cat

Pbk. Ed.
ISBN 1-55041-677-4

1. Kittens—Juvenile fiction. I. Cassidy, Sean, 1947- II. Title.

PS8575.L457C44 2001   jC813'.6   C2001-900581-4
PZ7.M22439Ch 2001

Fitzhenry & Whiteside acknowledges with thanks the Canada Council for the Arts, and the Ontario Arts Council for their support of our publishing program. We acknowledge the financial support of the Government of Canada through the Book Publishing Industry Development Program (BPIDP) for our publishing activities.

Cover and book design by Wycliffe Smith Design.

Printed in Hong Kong

The Chicken Cat

Merlin was born in a barn and raised by a chicken.
This was an odd turn of events for a cat, but the truth is,
Merlin never knew his real mother.

One dark, cold night in late winter, some thought they remembered a thin shadow waver in the barn's moonlight. When the yard erupted with the noisy chatter of first light, Merlin was found shivering and whining in a fistful of dirty hay. They called him Merlin because he appeared to have come to them through magic.

While Allison, the six-toed cat, was the obvious choice of adoptive mother, she barely gave Merlin a second glance. And so it was Guinevere, the oldest hen, who took the thin kitten under her wing.

You may have heard it said that chickens are not very bright. Well, I'm afraid there's some truth to this. But Guinevere knew enough to keep Merlin warm, and she sat on him well into that first day—until she could feel his shivering soften into a purr.

She begged a little milk from the two old goats, and clucked Merlin to sleep with a chicken lullaby.

Winter became spring, and while the other barn babies were born and grew up around him, Merlin barely grew at all. This was partly Guinevere's fault. While she loved Merlin like one of her own chicks, she really knew very little about raising a kitten. And it was partly the farmer's fault—the barn was cold and dark and dirty, and the single bag of dry feed was used to feed cow, cat and chicken alike. But partly it was just the way it was. Merlin's thin, feather-like fur concealed a fragile, birdlike frame.

By late spring, it was obvious to all the barn animals that Merlin wasn't doing well. His nose ran, and his eyes ran, and his scrawny little belly hurt with constant hunger. When Guinevere reached her wing around to cuddle Merlin close, he collapsed against her like crushed flowers.

All Merlin felt like doing was sleeping, but his sleep was restless and feverish.

During the day, he listened to Guinevere prattle and cluck. There was comfort in her chatter, and it surprised him to find that Guinevere had a dream. She told him that she longed to feel the wind lift her feathers and find herself floating on the air currents. Guinevere wanted to fly.

At night, he would watch Allison saunter into the middle of the barn and slowly stretch out her claws to reveal her prize. But as hungry as Merlin was, he had no appetite for the birds and mice she caught. He had a feeling he could easily be one of Allison's prizes if he wasn't careful.

Even though the weather got warmer, Merlin found himself cold all the time. He was still so thin that Guinevere could carry him around the barnyard tucked under her wing. But most of the time, she arranged her warm, flightless feathers around him almost as if she hoped to hatch him out of his sick little body. Merlin would snuggle in gratefully, and listen to her cluck on about her dreams of flying—her flights of fancy.

One morning, a child visited the barn—a little girl of five or six. The little girl wanted a kitten, but all the farmer could find was Allison, lounging in the shaft of sunlight which squeaked between the barn boards, and Allison was not a child's cat.

The farmer had forgotten about Merlin. Perhaps he never even knew Merlin existed. In any event, no one thought to look for a cat among the chickens.

With hazy curiosity, Merlin peeked out and watched them leave the barn.

Guinevere suddenly tucked him more closely against her generous body and started clucking in an agitated manner.

One minute he was buried in her feathers, struggling to keep his shivering body warm, the next Guinevere had picked him up in her beak and was running across the barnyard with him. She ran so fast she seemed almost to fly.

But the rush of open air and the rapid motion proved too much for Merlin, and he blacked out before he found himself deposited at the little girl's feet.

Merlin woke up to feel warm sunlight stroking his body.
He felt around for Guinevere, trying to feel her warm,
loving feathers. But when he opened his eyes, he was
nowhere that he knew. There was no busy barnyard prattle,
no cold, no chicken coop smell. Instead, he was curled
beside a window in a tangle of blankets with a small
child—a face he dimly recognized—asleep beside him.
Her arm cradled Merlin the way Guinevere's wing once did.

How long had he been here? How many days or weeks ago
had Guinevere clucked him to sleep with dreams about flying?

Merlin stretched out to a length he didn't know he possessed, and then rolled joyously onto his back. He missed Guinevere with an ache worse than hunger, but oh how good it felt to be warm and clean. How wonderful it felt to feel something other than pain in his belly.

He sat up to look out the window, and started when he realized how high up he was.

The window was an attic dormer on the third floor of an old house, and below him he could watch the little birds flit in the tree tops and dance across the roofs.

Merlin closed his eyes for a moment and tried to imagine Guinevere's wing still holding him close. He missed his chicken mother. He knew then that he had been born for Guinevere and she had been born for him.

He owed Guinevere his life two times over, and he yearned to give her something back.

As he watched the little birds outside the window, he suddenly knew what he must give her. He had a little knowledge to gain—the where and the how—but he knew in his heart that his desire would do the rest.

Over the summer, Merlin didn't grow much in size, but he did grow healthy and strong. He met Alfred, the humorless old tabby who also lived in the house. When Merlin danced around him in an invitation to play, Alfred scowled and growled and menaced. When Merlin did it again, Alfred drew back his clawless paw and sent him flying across the room. Merlin landed lightly, a little exhilarated by this unexpected flight.

In the days that followed, he'd sit for hours before the attic window thinking about how it felt when he was in mid-air —watching, waiting. By mid-August he was ready to hatch his plan.

On the hottest day in summer, the family had opened every window in the house. Merlin knew that this was the day, and he climbed to the attic window and looked out.

Without ceremony or fanfare, he stood by the open window and stretched himself up on his hind legs.

Closing his eyes, he took a deep breath . . . and jumped.

Merlin wavered only a second before he found a little air current above the tree tops.

While he'd never had the slightest doubt that he could do this, Merlin was still exhilarated by the freedom of flying.

Merlin smelled the barnyard before he saw it, but before too long, there it was below him.

He wasted no time in finding Guinevere who smiled and clucked excitedly. Merlin was excited, too.

They chased each other around the barnyard, Merlin concealing his secret until he had lured Guinevere to the top of the hen house.

As she paused to catch her breath, Merlin told her to grab hold of his tail with her beak. When she did so, he leapt onto the first little breeze that floated by and quickly rose above the tree tops with Guinevere flapping in wonder behind him.

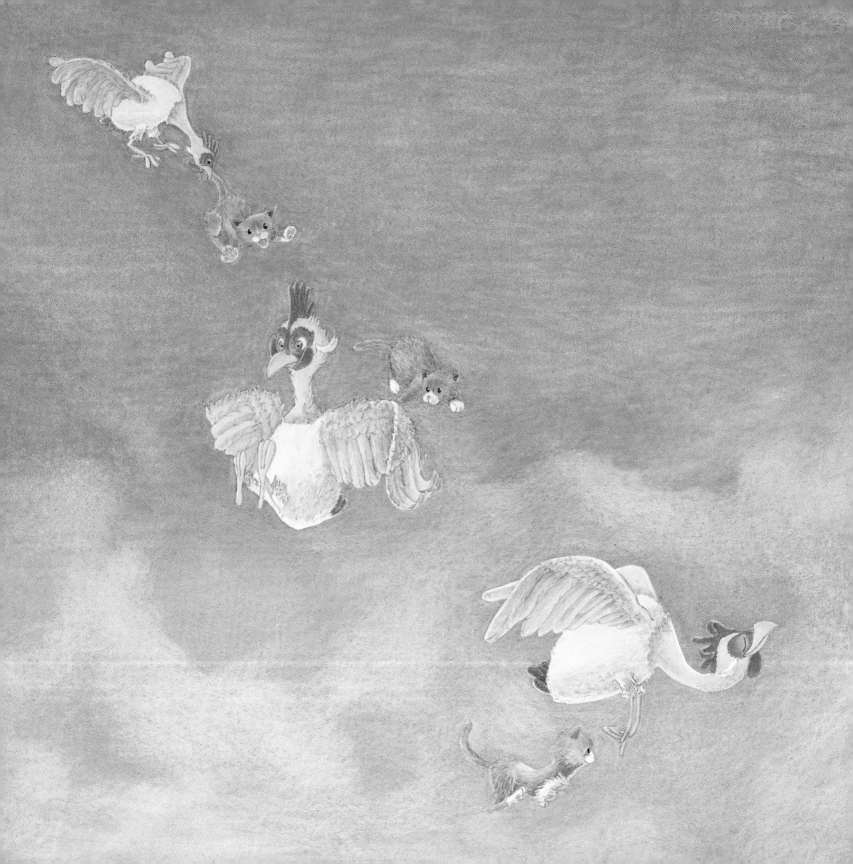

But as she slowly settled into the rhythm and wonder of Merlin's flight, Guinevere found that her very heart seemed to grow wings.

Together, they flew through the countryside until the moon crept up between the trees.

In the magic of the moonlight, they rested awhile in the highest branches of the highest tree.

Guinevere tucked Merlin briefly under her wing, and knew what he knew: that she had been born for Merlin, and Merlin had been born for her, and that, without a doubt, it was a strange but wonderful life.